Contents

A Play

The Talent Quest

Story by Jenny Giles

People in the Play

 Narrator

 Zoe

 Kylie

 Megan

 Luke

 Andrew

 Miss Bell

 Andrew's Mum

 Andrew's Dad

 Announcer

Narrator

Zoe, Kylie and Megan sang a song to the class.

Zoe, Kylie and Megan *(singing)*

There are different types of music.
Some are fast and some are slow.
Some will make you tap your feet,
And others gently flow.

People all around the world
Love to sing a song.
So if you like our music,
Please feel free to sing along.

Miss Bell

We all enjoyed listening to your song, girls. I think you should enter the Children's Talent Quest. It's going to be held at the Downtown Shopping Centre.

Megan

I'd be too nervous to sing at the shopping centre!

Kylie

No, you wouldn't, Megan. We'd be there to help you.

Zoe

We'll practise every day so that we'll be good enough.

Luke

A talent quest! You know, I can sing that song.

Andrew

So can I. My dad plays it on his guitar.

Kylie *(loudly)*

This is our song! We don't need you two.

Megan *(to Kylie)*

But it might sound better with some more voices.

Zoe

And they're both good singers …

Kylie

Well, I suppose we could see how it sounds.

Narrator

They all sang the song together.

Megan, Zoe, Kylie, Luke and Andrew *(singing)*

There are different types of music.
Some are fast and some are slow.
Some will make you tap your feet,
And others gently flow.

People all around the world
Love to sing a song.
So if you like our music,
Please feel free to sing along.

Miss Bell

That sounded even better than before!

Luke *(grinning)*

We made a big difference to the group, didn't we, Andrew?

Andrew

We all sang well together, so let's enter the talent quest.

Kylie

All right. Let's do it!

Narrator

The next day at school, Andrew had an idea.

Andrew

Mum says that you can come and practise at our place, and Dad says that he'll play his guitar for us to sing to.

Kylie

But wait a minute! Your dad won't be able to play for us at the talent quest. It's only for children.

Andrew

I know, but we're allowed to have a backing track, and Dad says he'll play our song through and record it.

Megan

And our song would sound much better with some music.

Narrator

So the following Saturday, they all went to Andrew's house to practise. They sang together while Andrew's dad played the guitar.

Narrator

Andrew's mum listened to them. She also had an idea!

Andrew's Mum

I could teach the girls how to sing a different melody for the last chorus, if you like. Then you could harmonise at the end of your song.

Andrew's Dad

That's a good idea. What do you all think?

Megan, Zoe, Kylie, Luke and Andrew *(nodding)*

Yes!

Narrator

The girls went into another room with Andrew's mum to learn the new melody, while the boys kept practising.

Soon, they were ready to try the song together. When they got to the last chorus, Andrew's mum gave the girls a signal, and they started to sing their melody.

But that made the boys go out of tune. They stopped singing, and the girls forgot their melody. Everyone started to laugh.

Luke *(groaning)*

That was terrible!

Megan

We'll never win if we sound like that!

Andrew's Dad

More practice needed!

Narrator

So they tried again, and again, and again … and then, at last, they got it right.

Megan, Zoe, Kylie, Luke and Andrew *(shouting)*

Hooray! We've done it!

Kylie

We can harmonise at last!

Andrew's Mum

And it sounded wonderful!

Narrator

On the day of the talent quest, the shopping centre was packed with people. Most of them were gathered around a stage that had been set up near the escalators.

Megan

Oh, no! Just look at the crowd! I can't sing in front of all these people!

Kylie

Of course you can, Megan. We'll be up there with you.

Narrator

The children were shown where to go, and told that they were last on the program. They sat down and waited for the first item to begin.

A small girl played the violin, and after that an older girl sang.

Then, a boy began to play the piano, and the crowd fell silent as the beautiful music echoed through the centre.

Andrew *(whispering)*

He was very good.

Narrator

The boy took a bow and the audience applauded loudly. The children listened to some more performers, and then, at last, the announcer beckoned to them.

Narrator

Kylie and Zoe looked at Megan. Then they took her by the hand, and the five children went up onto the stage.

They could see hundreds of people. There were faces gazing down at them from upstairs and faces staring up at them from below the stage.

Zoe *(in a nervous voice)*

Help! I'm nervous now!

Megan *(in a nervous voice)*

Well, I'm terrified, and my voice is going all shaky!

Luke *(in a nervous voice)*

I think I've forgotten the song!

Kylie

Hey! Look down there in the front row.

Narrator

They all looked down at the crowd.

And there, in the front seats, they could see Miss Bell and some of the boys and girls from their class. They were smiling and waving at them.

Kylie

Come on! We can do it!

Narrator

They clipped on their microphones and began to sing.

The audience listened in silence as the clear notes of the song rang out.

Narrator

The children came to the last chorus and began to sing the two melodies together. They harmonised perfectly, and when they reached the end of the song, the audience clapped and cheered and whistled loudly.

The crowd was still applauding when the announcer came up onto the stage.

Announcer *(smiling and holding up his hands to stop the clapping)*

The judges have had a very difficult decision to make, and I would like Josef, who played the piano so well, to come up onto the stage.

Announcer

And now, here they are … the joint winners of this year's Children's Talent Quest … Josef, and the group who just sang to us … Zoe … Megan … Kylie … Luke … and Andrew!

Narrator

The children smiled excitedly at each other while the crowd clapped and cheered again.

Announcer *(to the crowd)*

Now, let's hear that song again from our winning group, and perhaps you may like to join in, too!

Megan, Zoe, Kylie, Luke and Andrew *(singing)*

There are different types of music.
Some are fast and some are slow.
Some will make you tap your feet,
And others gently flow.

People all around the world
Love to sing a song.
So if you like our music,
Please feel free to sing along.

A Play

Rory's Big Chance

Story by Krista Bell

People in the Play

Narrator

Rory

Simon

Rory's Dad

Jill

Narrator

Rory and his father walked into the television studio.

Rory

I hope I get this part! It could be my big chance!

Narrator

Rory had been to auditions before, but today he felt nervous. He loved acting in advertisements and, so far, he'd been chosen to do a few small parts. But what he really wanted was the chance to play a leading role.

TELEVISION
TV
STUDIO

Narrator

Rory and Dad went into the waiting room. Simon, the casting agent, met them there.

Simon

Hello, Rory. It's good to see you again. Sit with the others, and I'll let you know when it's your turn.

Narrator

Several other children had arrived ahead of Rory, and he knew that he was going to have a long wait.

One by one, the children went into the studio to be auditioned. Rory watched them smiling happily at their parents as they left the waiting room.

Rory *(whispering to Dad)*

I'm really nervous. I don't think I've got a chance.

Rory's Dad

You'll be just fine. It'll be your turn soon.

Narrator

Just then, Simon opened the door.

Simon *(smiling)*

You can come with me now, Rory.

Narrator

Rory took a deep breath and followed Simon into a big room, where a woman was adjusting a video camera.

Simon

This is Jill. She's going to be directing the advertisement.

Jill

Hello, Rory. Simon has told me that you're very good at acting and singing, and I've seen your last ad. You did a great job, and I'm sure you would enjoy this one. It's about a marvellous new pen called the Wobblenot. The pen has been designed to help children write quickly and neatly.

Rory *(laughing)*

I'd like to have a pen that would help me do neater work!

Jill

For this ad, we want you to pretend that you've got a lot of homework, and you're having trouble doing it neatly. You're tired, and you begin to dream about a pen that would help you improve your writing. You sing a little jingle, and the Wobblenot appears, dancing across your page. It jumps into your hand, and you wake up.

Simon

Then you use the pen to do the neatest homework ever!

Narrator

Rory knew that he would be able to do the ad. He looked through the script that Simon handed him, and he stopped feeling nervous.

Jill taught Rory the jingle that he would have to sing for his audition. Then she told him to sit behind a small desk.

Simon

When you're ready, we'll make a video recording of you.

Rory *(quietly to himself)*

This is my big chance to show them what I can do!

Narrator

Rory followed the script carefully. He sang the jingle, and imagined the pen jumping into his hand. Then he held up his neatly written homework, and read it to the camera.

Jill wrote something on her notepad.

Rory *(singing)*

This pen is called a Wobblenot.
It helps you write more neatly.
You'll get your work done quicker,
And you'll finish it completely.

This pen will dance across your page.
Just watch it loop and swirl.
It's a pen that should be owned
By every boy and girl.

Jill

That was great! Thanks for coming. We'll let you know tomorrow if you've been chosen for the part.

Narrator

Rory walked back out to the waiting room.

Rory's Dad

How did you go?

Rory

I think it was okay. I'd really love to get the part.

Narrator

Simon rang the next morning.

Simon

I've got some great news for you, Rory! We were very happy with your audition. We want you to do the ad for us!

Rory

That's brilliant! Thanks, Simon.

Simon

We'll be filming the ad next Saturday. Make sure you practise your lines, and the jingle, too!

Rory

I will!

Narrator

During that week, Rory learned all of his lines. He practised them over and over again. He sang the jingle in the shower, and on his way to school. He even sang it to Oscar, his dog!

Rory *(singing)*

This pen is called a Wobblenot.
It helps you write more neatly.
You'll get your work done quicker,
And you'll finish it completely.

This pen will dance across your page.
Just watch it loop and swirl.
It's a pen that should be owned
By every boy and girl.

Narrator

By Thursday evening, Rory was word-perfect. He put on his skates, and went up and down the path, singing the jingle once more.

Oscar heard Rory singing, and came racing excitedly around the corner of the house.

Rory swerved to avoid him, but he lost his balance. He staggered and wobbled off the path, and then skidded into the fence!

Rory's dad heard the crash, and ran out to the backyard.

Rory's Dad

Rory! Are you okay?

Rory *(gasping)*

My ankle is really hurting.

Rory's Dad

Let me look at your ankle … I think it might be broken. I'm going to phone for an ambulance.

Narrator

That evening, Rory lay on the couch, looking at the plaster on his leg.

Rory *(miserably)*

I won't be able to make the ad now.

Rory's Dad

Cheer up. There'll be other ads. I'll have to phone Simon, and let him know what's happened.

Rory

No other ad will be as good as this one. It was my big chance, and now I've lost it!

Narrator

Rory listened to his dad as he told Simon what had happened. There was a long silence, and then …

Rory's Dad *(in an excited voice)*

That's fantastic! I'll let Rory know.

Rory

Fantastic? What's so fantastic, Dad?

Rory's Dad

Simon and Jill still want you to do the ad!

Rory

But how can I? I can't even walk properly!

Rory's Dad

You'll just be sitting behind a desk, so it won't matter that your ankle is in plaster. And besides, they think you're the best person for the job.

Narrator

On Saturday, Rory sat behind the desk in the studio. The cameras began to roll, and suddenly he felt very confident. He went right through the ad, singing and acting the part perfectly. He didn't forget a single line.

Simon

Well done! This is going to be a great advertisement!

Rory *(grinning)*

And I got my big chance after all!